A New Year to Love

By
Ruth Bawell

Table of Contents

Unsolicited Testimonials.............. 4

FREE GIFT............................. 5

CHAPTER ONE........................... 6

CHAPTER TWO.......................... 12

CHAPTER THREE........................ 26

CHAPTER FOUR......................... 36

CHAPTER FIVE......................... 44

CHAPTER SIX.......................... 57

FREE GIFT............................ 63

Please Check out My Other Works...... 64

Thank You............................ 65

Unsolicited Testimonials

By **Phyllis**

⭐⭐⭐⭐⭐ **Love Ruth!**

I love Ruth's books! Her mysteries are the best!

⭐⭐⭐⭐⭐ **Love This Author**

Ruth Bawell is very creative and a great writer! All her books have left me unable to stop reading till the ending! There were a few Amish fact mistakes, like unmarried man having a beard, but the plot was so good I overlooked that!

By **Steve M**

⭐⭐⭐⭐⭐ **I love romance stories** August 5, 2017
I love romance stories... well written with her usual twists to the story still enjoyed them very much Once I start I can't put it down.

By **Bones**

⭐⭐⭐⭐⭐ **Amish County Stories**
I love all the Amish County stories! Each one brings so much excitement! Ruth Bawell is also a wonderful writer!

By **Kindle Customer**

⭐⭐⭐⭐⭐ **Good clean writing.**
The Amish stories of Ruth Bawell are authentic, faith-filled writings. They are short, more the length of novellas or longer short stories. Always clean, always uplifting.

CHAPTER ONE

"*Gute mariye*, Becca!" Naomi Ropp greeted her neighbor Rebecca Weaver, peering over the stall at Naomi's back as she was milking a cow in the dairy shed.

"*Gute mariye* to you too, Naomi," Becca replied, turning around briefly and flashing her friend a bright smile. "What brings you around so early in the day?"

"I need to borrow some eggs, Becca," Naomi said, stifling a yawn. "With our house filled with visiting family members of all ages, I can scarcely keep tabs on what we have and what we don't, and run out of things before I can get to the mercantile. We really should keep chickens like you do. It's so convenient."

"That's what neighbors are for, my dear," Becca laughed. "To keep chickens so you don't have to. I just fetched some eggs from the chicken coop, and they're in the kitchen, so take as many as you like."

"Thank you, Becca," Naomi said, turning to leave. She turned back, her forehead furrowed. "Did little Simon sleep over at your house last night? I'm losing track, with all the children and adults around."

Becca laughed. "Yes, he did," she replied, leaning back on her milking stool and brushing the back of her hand across her brow as she swiveled around to face Naomi. "He and our Mark have been inseparable since your extended family arrived. It's quite beautiful to see, actually, how the two bond, despite Mark being only four years old and Simon almost six. But yes, I'm losing track of time and days, as we have all been occupied every moment."

"We've had a busy Christmas, haven't we?" Naomi observed. "And yesterday was just wonderful."

"Yes, it was! Though it's always a little sad when Christmas is over," Becca replied. "Especially since…"

Naomi walked over to her friend and slid a comforting arm around her shoulder.

"I understand. The get-togethers during the holidays keep you from thinking of David, and after it's over…"

Becca sighed. "I'm just glad that Mark isn't missing his father the way I do," she said.

"He was just two years old when David passed," Naomi replied, "so I guess in a way it's easier for him… but I do feel for you, Becca. You lost your husband when you were just twenty-three, and you're only twenty-five years old now. I can only imagine how hard it must be for you."

"Don't feel sorry for me, Naomi," Becca said. "I have a lot to be grateful for. Just having you all next door, for instance, has helped me tremendously." She rose from her milking stool and moved to the next cow.

"I guess I had better go and fix breakfast," Naomi said. She paused and turned to Becca again. "And don't forget, we have to get ready for New Year's Eve! Should we discuss the menu while the children are busy playing games today?"

"Where are the games to be?" Becca queried, looking up.

"At your house, of course," Naomi chuckled. "Ours is just too full!"

"Alright, then," Becca replied, "we can discuss the menu over pie and hot chocolate, but one of us will have to watch the children."

"And I know you love to," Naomi said, "but we need your attention while we discuss the menu, so maybe we'll get the older kids to watch the younger ones."

"Good idea," Becca replied with a laugh. "See you soon! Oh, and you can wake Simon. He will need to go back to your house to wash and change."

"I will," Naomi replied. "His *daed* has been looking all over for him."

"Like I mentioned," Becca said, "he and Mark have been inseparable. I suppose it must be hard for Simon to have lost his *mamm* so young. It must be hard for his *daed* too."

"My dear cousin Isaac struggled at first, but he's getting better at being a single parent now," Naomi replied.

She frowned. "Or is he?" she murmured to herself as she left the Weaver's dairy shed.

After Naomi left, Rebecca resumed milking, even as her mind drifted back to the events of the past year that was now drawing to a close. It hadn't been easy, losing her husband so young, and if it hadn't been for her family and good neighbors, she wouldn't have been able to manage bringing her son Mark up on her own. She smiled to herself as she thought of the previous weeks leading up to Christmas. The days had been filled with cooking and taking care of all the children as the Weavers and Ropps came together to celebrate the Season, affording Becca a brief respite from the loneliness she experienced each day as a very young widow.

She was still deep in thought as she walked back to the house, carrying a pail of milk, when she saw Naomi leaving with Simon. Her heart went out to the little boy. To lose a mother when he needed one the most was harsh indeed, she thought to herself. No wonder he clung to her whenever he came to play with Mark. She hoped that his father was not neglecting him. She had no idea which of the Ropp men he was, because when Simon was not at the Weaver's home, he was with Naomi and her mother.

"Becca!" her mother, Priscilla, said, as she set the pail down in the kitchen, "Don't forget that we have invited the Ropps to supper this evening."

"Really?" Becca replied, her brow furrowed. "I just met Naomi and she didn't mention anything."

"That's probably because she assumed that you remembered we had planned it several days ago," Priscilla answered. She looked anxiously at her daughter. "Are you alright, my dear?"

"Perhaps I'm just a little tired, *Mamm*," Becca replied with a sigh. "And to be honest, it's that time of year when I wish the Holidays didn't have to end," she added, "because that's when all the feelings of hopelessness come rushing back."

"May the New Year be a better one, Becca, my child," Priscilla whispered, giving her daughter a hug.

"I wouldn't have got through any of the past years after David if it hadn't been for you and *Daed, Mamm*," Becca whispered back, feeling the comfort of her mother's arms envelop her.

"I think this moment calls for a mug of hot chocolate, scrambled eggs and oven-toasted bread, don't you?" Priscilla said.

Becca nodded and smiled. "Except that Naomi was here a short while ago, and I told her to take as many eggs as she wanted."

"Which was all of them," Priscilla laughed.

"Race you to the chicken coop," Becca said, running out of the kitchen door, with her mother close behind her, both women holding their *kaaps* down on their heads as the winter breeze threatened to blow them off. And moments later, as Priscilla and Becca rummaged for eggs in the chicken coop, surrounded by the clucking of hens and the warm earthy smell of the coop, Becca felt a sense of peace slip over her shoulders like a warm blanket.

CHAPTER TWO

Isaac Ropp looked out from the house next door to the Weavers'. He caught a brief glimpse of Becca running towards the chicken coop with Priscilla following close behind. Both women were laughing as they ran, and the sight took Isaac back to another time and the sound of another laugh—that of his late wife, Eva.

Momentarily engulfed by a wave of sadness, Isaac stepped away from the window and covered his face with his hands. It had been difficult bringing Simon up without a mother, and it was only because his own mother had stepped in to help that he had been able to cope.

"But a *groosmammi* isn't a *mamm*," Isaac said aloud, "beloved though a *groosmammi* is."

"Isaac?" Naomi called, looking in, "are you alright?"

Isaac slid his hands off his face. "Yes," he replied, averting his gaze.

"I'm sorry," Naomi said. "This time of year can't be easy."

"Where's Simon?" Isaac asked, swiftly changing the subject.

"I just fetched him from next door," Naomi replied.

"Now that's another problem," Isaac remarked, taking his hat off and raking his fingers through his thick dark hair.

"Sorry, do you not approve of Simon staying over next door?" Naomi queried in surprise.

"Oh no, no," Isaac said hurriedly. "I didn't mean that. On the contrary, I am so glad that Simon has had company over the holidays. But he keeps mentioning that he wished for a brother. Now he has gotten one, and that bothers me because I wonder what we will do when he has to be separated from Mark."

"I'm sure once you all are back home, Simon will get busy with school and forget Mark," Naomi declared.

"Perhaps, and perhaps not," Isaac replied. "What I don't want is for him to suffer the trauma of separation yet again."

"We will all pray that he won't," Naomi said. "Simon has been through a lot these past years, and so have you, Isaac."

"These past weeks have been wonderful, Naomi, thank you," Isaac replied. "Just getting together with family and friends has been a much-needed respite." He smiled. "And seeing Simon happy has been the best thing ever. You know, I don't think I have ever seen him like this."

"I suppose you have Mark to thank," Naomi chuckled.

"How old is he?" Isaac asked.

"Just four years old, and he and Simon have bonded because each of these two little boys has lost a parent," Naomi said.

"What?" Isaac queried. "Lost a parent? Mark?"

"Didn't you know?" Naomi asked. "Mark lost his *daed* two years ago."

"Oh, dear, I had no idea," Isaac replied. "How very sad."

"It is," Naomi said. "Mark's *mamm* has had a difficult time, as well."

"I don't think I've met her," Isaac remarked. "Despite the fact that our families have been together for the holidays."

"You most definitely have met Mark's *mamm*," Naomi replied. "Her name is Rebecca… Becca, and she's my best friend."

Isaac shrugged. "Forgive me, I don't recall meeting her, and I can only say that's because I have just been so preoccupied."

"That's alright," Naomi said. "It's understandable. Only moments ago, Becca was telling me how hard this time of year is, but for different reasons. She is always sad when

Christmas is over, because being busy and around so many people helps her overcome her own feelings of grief and loss."

"It's strange how submerged we are in our own misery that we fail to realize others are suffering around us, many with smiles on their faces," Isaac remarked.

"You have aptly described Becca," Naomi said. "She is always smiling, because she never wants Mark to see her sad if she can help it."

A thought crossed Naomi's mind. "Would you like to watch the children while they play games next door today?" she asked.

"I wouldn't mind, but isn't that task assigned to all the ladies?" Isaac replied.

"Yes, we never bother the menfolk with supervising the children," Naomi declared. "Except today when us ladies need to concentrate on discussing the menu for New Year's Eve."

"Ah," Isaac murmured with an amused grin, "that's a very important task for sure, and we menfolk need to do all we can to ensure that nothing hampers the discussion and planning of a menu."

"Stop teasing me," Naomi protested. "This is serious."

"I know," Isaac declared. "And I wasn't teasing you. I just love the way everyone in Cloverfield Village takes the holidays so seriously. All the events, planning and preparations are impressive, and we have enjoyed every minute of them."

"So you'll help watch the children?" Naomi asked.

"If I can bring your dear husband along to help me," Isaac answered.

"Joshua?" Naomi queried uncertainly. She shrugged. "He hasn't had any experience, unfortunately."

"I'm sorry," Isaac apologized hastily. "I didn't mean to touch a nerve."

"It's alright," Naomi said with a sigh. "We've been married for five years with no children, and Joshua is somewhat hesitant whenever I suggest he help out with any. I think it's because it reminds him that we don't have our own."

"You both are so young," Isaac observed, "and I don't think you should write off your chances of having children someday soon."

Naomi sighed. "I suppose that's why we make so much of the holidays. All of us being together helps us forget whatever is missing in our lives," she declared.

"May the New Year bring you what you most desire, cousin," Isaac said.

"I wish the same for you, Isaac," Naomi replied. "And you should definitely get Joshua to help you supervise the children's games today. He needs a taste of what he is missing."

Later, Isaac went to the Weavers' house, accompanied by Naomi's husband Joshua and all the children belonging to the Ropp family.

"So Josh," Isaac began, "have you any ideas for children's games? We could play Jenga and Pictionary, inside by the fire," Isaac suggested. "But it is such a nice day, and the children have been cooped up. What do you think?"

Joshua shrugged. "I grew up playing outside and don't really know any of those new board games. I'm just here to help you keep the little ones entertained. But I was thinking, maybe we could get everyone wrapped up nice and warm and build a snowman or two outside."

"That's a good idea," Isaac said, nodding and smiling to himself at the idea of Jenga being a 'new' game to Joshua. "We've plenty of snow too."

"*Daed*!" Simon cried excitedly, running to Isaac, "are you going to play with us today?"

"Yes, and so is your *Onkel* Josh," Isaac replied.

"I can see that we aren't being missed at all," Becca sighed, looking at the children out in the yard building a snowman with Isaac and Joshua. "Especially since we would have insisted on the kids being indoors by the fire, playing tame board games."

"Simon is so excited," Naomi observed. "And so is Mark. I'm glad we had a menu to plan. I guess the kids needed this." She patted Becca on her shoulder. "And they need us too, don't you fret. We're the ones who fix the tasty meals and make them hot chocolate and cookies at the drop of a hat," she added.

"It takes a man and a woman together to bring up a child," Becca replied. "One cannot supplant the other in a child's affections. So no, I'm not fretting. In fact, it's nice to have a day to sit together and plan a meal, uninterrupted."

A loud howl of pain drew her attention back to the children outside.

"What happened?" she cried in alarm.

"I'll go and check," Naomi said. "You all keep going with the menu planning. We need to prepare the best New Year's Eve feast ever." She looked out of the window and turned to Becca. "Don't get alarmed, but it seems like Mark has hurt himself."

"What? Oh, no!" Becca exclaimed, rushing out of the door and almost colliding with Isaac. He was coming in carrying Mark, with Simon following anxiously.

"What happened?" Becca cried.

"It's alright. Mark is fine," Isaac answered. "He just got a snowball thrown at him and he wasn't used to it, so he was startled."

"Why you men always have to suggest rough games, I'll never understand!" Becca exclaimed. "There really was no need to be outdoors when we had all the games laid out here."

"I understand that you might be distressed, but there's no need to be," Isaac replied. "Mark is fine."

"I'm fine, *Mamm*," Mark said, sliding out of Isaac's arms and running to Becca.

"Boys shouldn't be coddled and kept indoors," Isaac declared. "One day Mark will be grown and will need to be out in the cold chopping wood or driving his buggy to market in the snow, and then…" He stopped. "My apologies. It's really none of my business."

"We haven't met," Becca declared coldly.

"This is my *daed*," Simon said, taking Mark's hand and leading him back into the snow outside.

"Considering you've barely been seen around your son, it's a wonder that you consider yourself to be in a position to hand out parenting advice," Becca declared hotly and turned away from Isaac.

"What just happened?" Naomi queried. "You were rather too harsh with Isaac."

"I know he's your cousin, Naomi," Becca replied. "But he was trying to give me parenting advice, which I didn't take kindly to, given the tone which he adopted. And considering he compromised the safety of our children by taking them out into the snow."

"Isaac is a single parent just like you, Becca," Naomi said, "and he's also a responsible person. He wouldn't compromise the safety of any of the children. I think you overreacted just now."

Becca chewed on her lower lip. "I'm sorry," she said, "but your cousin doesn't appear to be the most hands-on *daed*, and yet he was giving *me* advice on how to raise Mark… talking as if I wasn't doing a good job of being a mother…"

"You're a wonderful *mamm* to Mark, Becca," Naomi said, "and Isaac is a good *daed* to Simon. I'm sure neither of you intends hurting the other or casting aspersions on each other's parenting skills. And I apologize on Isaac's behalf for inadvertently hurting your feelings."

"I'm sorry," a voice spoke from the doorway, and Becca looked up to see Isaac standing there looking embarrassed. "I didn't mean any harm and…"

"It's alright," Becca replied. "I'm sorry too, for overreacting."

She looked at Isaac, overcome with compassion for him and Simon. "I truly am sorry," she said.

"*Mamm*!" Mark cried excitedly from behind Isaac. "We built a snowmamm!"

"I think you mean *snowman*!" Becca laughed, swinging Mark up into her arms and kissing his pink cheeks.

Isaac looked at her, noticing her for the first time—her cornflower blue eyes and honey-gold hair, delicate features and warm smile.

"Let's go and see your snowman, Mark," Becca said, stepping outside with her son in her arms. When Naomi followed, along with the other women who had all been intently planning the New Year's Eve Supper menu, something magical took place, and soon all the mothers and their children were throwing snowballs at each other, as Isaac and Joshua watched amusedly from the sidelines.

"That was fun," Becca declared.

"It was," Naomi agreed, brushing snowflakes off her hair and clothes. "Except that we will all need to change our clothes if we don't want to catch cold."

"But the menu isn't fully planned yet," Becca observed.

"I think we have a sufficient number of dishes on it, and now all we need to do is figure out who cooks what," Naomi said.

Outside, still in the snow with the children, Isaac watched Simon and Mark play together after the womenfolk went indoors. His attention was momentarily diverted by the sight of Becca as she stepped onto the porch to look outside. Something had stirred within him as he had watched her, moments before, romping in the snow with the children. For just a while, she had been like a child herself, all cares thrust aside as she enjoyed something she so obviously had never enjoyed before. And, as the sheer joy of abandoning herself to the allure of the snow transformed her, her face glowed, her smile was radiant. Her laughter filled the air, rising and falling like sweet notes of a melody. He had been enthralled then, and he was captivated now, not realizing that Joshua was watching him with a strange look in his eyes.

"Isaac," Joshua said, inclining his head in the direction of the Weavers' porch where Becca stood watching the children. "Do you see what I see?"

"Children in the snow," Isaac replied, his voice hushed, as he turned his attention back to Mark, Simon and the other children.

"Yes," Joshua replied, "but *what else* do you see?"

"I don't know," Isaac answered. "Is there something I'm missing?"

"I hope you aren't missing it," Joshua murmured. "Because this could be the answer to all our prayers."

"What?" Isaac asked. "What are you saying, Josh?"

"You figure it out, Isaac," Joshua said, his voice solemn. "You figure it out and then go and do something about it."

For a while Isaac just stood there, still overcome by that vision of responsible mothers discovering the children within themselves. But one mother had captured his gaze almost completely. She stirred so many emotions within him: compassion, amazement, awe, sadness, joy. How did a woman like Becca survive the pain of losing a husband when she was so young, he wondered. How did she find the strength each day to get out of bed, do her chores and care for her son?

And then, he realized, those were the same questions he was asking of himself. How had he gone through the past three years without his dear wife, Eva? His eyes filled with tears, as they so often did when he thought of Simon's mother, gone too soon. And then the echo of Becca's laughter in the snow returned, and he smiled.

He remembered how her face had been bathed in an almost divine light when she looked upon her child. He thought of how his own face must have mirrored the same emotions when he gazed upon his son, aware that, no matter what, for this one person, he must keep going.

CHAPTER THREE

"*Daed*," Simon said, "I want to ride with Mark and his *mamm*, please."

Isaac looked down at his son, who was clutching his hand and gazing beseechingly up at him. The Ropp and Weaver families were going on a sleigh ride in the snow, driving up to Cloverfield's frozen lake, which had recently been pronounced safe for ice skating.

"Of course you may, son," Isaac replied, giving Simon's hand a reassuring squeeze.

"I want you to come too," Simon said.

"Of course I'm coming, son," Isaac answered. "I'll be right behind you in another sleigh."

"No, this sleigh," Simon said firmly, pointing to a sleigh already occupied by Mark, Becca and three other children.

"There doesn't seem to be enough room for us," Isaac murmured. "Though you could squeeze in."

"*Daed*, will you come with me, please?" Simon entreated.

"Alright, son," Isaac replied, walking bravely up to the sleigh, in which Becca had been seated only a minute before. She had jumped off now, and was helping more children into it, so that by the time they took off, the sleigh appeared to be filled with children of varied ages, with Becca and Isaac just about visible amidst them all.

Becca began to sing, and the children followed suit. Isaac felt Simon nudge him.

"Sing, *Daed*," he said.

And most self-consciously, Isaac began to sing.

Becca, who was in the seat in front, turned around briefly to flash him a smile of encouragement, but after that, appeared to be oblivious of his presence as she concentrated on keeping the children entertained during the ride.

"I see that you've taken my advice and are doing something about *it*," Joshua whispered to Isaac, giving him a mysterious look as they arrived at the lake.

"Doing something about *what*?" Isaac queried, looking mystified.

"Come on, Isaac," Joshua said, inclining his head towards the spot where Becca stood, surrounded by a group of children. "I think I know the direction your thoughts are taking."

"*What*?" Isaac said. "Josh, whatever do you mean?"

"Well, all I can say is, I'm with you, Isaac. It was a good start, riding in the sleigh with all the children," Joshua replied.

"Simon insisted that I did," Isaac said wryly. "And he wanted to ride in the same sleigh as Mark."

"Simon told Naomi—more than once, I might add—that he wished for a brother as a Christmas gift, and he found Mark," Joshua declared.

"My dear friend and cousin-in-law," Isaac replied, "we must not speak of such matters lightly."

"And I don't," Joshua replied. "I don't take any of this lightly. And I hope you see that the hand of the Lord is on this situation, and that you must do something about it."

"I cannot," Isaac said.

"Why not?" Joshua countered.

"This could just be fanciful thinking. And how can I, still not over the tragedy in my life, even think of pursuing an alliance with someone who isn't over the tragedy in her own life?"

"I saw the way you were watching her the other day," Joshua remarked.

"It wasn't what you thought it was, Josh," Isaac replied. "I'm sorry to disappoint you."

"So you don't feel anything for the person in question?" Joshua asked.

"Only compassion and understanding. I know exactly what she must be going through, because that's what I am dealing with," Isaac replied.

"So, in other words, you both have something significant in common with each other," Joshua persisted.

"How can the tragedies that we have each endured actually bring us together?" Isaac queried.

"Pray about it," Joshua said. "And now it's time to take the children out across the lake and hope that it is indeed safe for skating."

"I'm glad to see you more willing to help out with the children," Isaac observed.

Joshua shrugged. "I guess the other day in the snow changed my outlook a little." He gave Isaac a knowing smile. "And maybe it changed your outlook too."

Ahead of them, Becca had already gotten Mark and Simon into their skates, and she and Naomi were gingerly picking their way onto the frozen surface of the lake.

"Thank goodness," Becca breathed when Isaac and Joshua took Mark and Simon to skate with them. "I was just being brave, but I honestly am much happier not skating."

"Then come and help me organize refreshments for everyone at the Lakeside Café," Naomi said.

"This is fun," Becca remarked, as they trudged through the snow.

"It might be," Naomi agreed with a vigorous nod, "if I didn't feel quite so nauseous."

"Was it something you ate?" Becca queried absently.

"We all ate exactly the same food, so I don't know what could possibly have disagreed with me," Naomi sighed. She stopped and clutched her temples. "And I feel strangely lightheaded."

"Come into the Café and sit down," Becca said, taking her friend's arm. "It's been a busy Season, and you are probably just exhausted."

"May we have some hot chocolate, please?" Becca asked the lady at the counter. "My friend here is feeling lightheaded and nauseous, and it could be that she didn't have enough breakfast, or maybe the sleigh ride caused it."

"Or maybe, like me, she is feeling all the effects of pregnancy," the lady at the counter said, leaning closer to Becca.

"Pregnancy?" Becca queried. She shook her head. "My friend has been married for five years and hasn't had any children, so I doubt…"

"Never doubt the gifts of the Lord, child," the lady said. She set two mugs of steaming hot chocolate on the counter and slid a plate of cookies across to Becca. "You take care of your friend. Don't let her exert too much, and first chance that you get, have her do a pregnancy test. That is, if she hasn't already done one and is saving the news to surprise you with at an appropriate time."

"Naomi," Becca said solemnly, sitting down opposite her friend, "is there anything that you want to tell me? After all, we are best friends, aren't we?"

"Becca, yes, there is something," Naomi replied, nodding solemnly. "It's been on my mind so much, and I've wanted to tell you on several occasions these past days, but Joshua didn't want me to tell you until we were certain that it was what we hoped it may be."

"And is it what you hoped it may be?" Becca asked.

"It could be," Naomi replied.

"Did you check?" Becca queried.

"Not personally, no," Naomi answered.

"Then how did you check?" Becca asked, her brow furrowed. "Did you ask someone who knows about these things?"

"Joshua asked the person concerned," Naomi answered, reaching for her hot chocolate, and then holding her hand up to her mouth to suppress a gag.

"Naomi, you can speak plainly. I'm your friend," Becca said.

"As a friend, I think I should wait before speaking, because I need to be certain," Naomi said.

"I can see the signs," Becca remarked, looking closely at her friend.

"You can?" Naomi responded. "Why, that's wonderful, Becca! I'm happy for you!"

"Happy for *me*? I'm happy for *you*, Naomi!" Becca exclaimed.

"We all will be happy when it comes to fruition," Naomi declared.

"How long will that be?" Becca asked. "Eight months? Six months?"

"It depends on how soon you want it to happen, I guess," Naomi answered.

Becca wrinkled her brow in confusion. "What exactly are you talking about, Naomi?" she asked.

Naomi gave her friend a wary glance and adjusted her *kaap* over her hair. "What are *you* talking about, Becca?" she countered.

"I hope we are talking about the same thing," Becca answered, still looking confused.

Naomi reached for her mug of hot chocolate again, and her hand flew to her mouth once more, as the lady from the counter came running up to them.

"Just nibble on a cookie, dear, and it will pass. Believe me, I had morning sickness for all of my five children and it wasn't the most pleasant part of being pregnant."

"Pregnant? No, I'm not pregnant," Naomi declared.

"Have you gained weight?" the woman queried. "Is your gown a bit tighter, and are your apron strings feeling like they're somehow shorter?"

Naomi's hand flew to her mouth. "It's holiday weight, isn't it? All those pies, turkey, roast pork… cakes…"

"So you've found that your appetite has increased, haven't you?" the lady asked.

"Everyone's does during the holidays," Naomi replied.

"My dear, you are carrying a little one in your belly, or my name's not Mercy Troyer," the lady declared vehemently.

"We are happy to meet you, Mercy Troyer," Naomi said. "But please know this: I have been married for five years and don't have any children. If you raise my hopes, they will be crushed."

"If you don't trust what I just said, trust in the Lord, child," Mercy replied. "Now go and get yourself a checkup as soon as you possibly can, and you're welcome to a mug of hot chocolate on the house when you return to tell me I was right." Mercy smiled and walked back to the kitchen.

"Before Mercy came to our table to tell you that you are pregnant," Becca said, "you were saying that you wanted to tell me something. What is it?"

"I daresay Joshua was right, and I shouldn't say anything until we have more facts to go on," Naomi replied. "And also, I am now really set on getting to a doctor for a checkup."

"So you won't tell me what you were talking about so mysteriously?" Becca asked.

"Maybe later," Naomi said.

"What's wrong with Naomi?" Joshua asked Becca as the skaters trooped into the Café. "She looks unwell."

"I think she should probably see a doctor right away," Becca replied.

"Oh, dear, I hope it's nothing serious," Joshua said.

"It's probably just something she ate," Becca smiled.

"She is holding her belly and looking alarmed," Joshua remarked, looking concerned.

"The moment we get back, you must see a doctor," Becca replied.

CHAPTER FOUR

Becca brushed her hair and then sat down on the edge of her bed, gazing at Mark fast asleep on the bed next to hers, with Simon right beside him. The two boys had been inseparable as they ice skated and later played in the snow with Isaac and Joshua. It had been a memorable day indeed, what with Naomi feeling unwell and a stranger called Mercy Troyer telling her that she was with child. Naomi couldn't wait to see a doctor, but when they got back and went in search of one, they were told that the local medic was away for the holidays.

"We will have to go to town, to a proper hospital," Naomi told Becca, "and I can scarcely wait, as I am so eager to know if what Mercy Troyer said is true."

Becca smiled to herself at the thought of Naomi finally becoming a mother. Still, she was equally curious to know what Naomi had wanted to tell her, but hadn't.

The sound of a motor car sent her to the window, and she leaned out, just about able to see that a cab had pulled up outside the Ropps' house.

Becca hurriedly put on her *kaap* and threw a shawl around her shoulders as she ran down the stairs and out of the front door.

"Naomi!" she cried, pounding on the door. "Is something wrong?"

It was Isaac who opened the door to her.

"Becca, come inside," he said. "It's freezing outdoors."

"The cab," Becca said. "Is something wrong?"

"Naomi has to be taken to the hospital in town," Isaac replied. "She has been feeling very unwell and throwing up a lot."

"Should I go with her?" Becca asked, looking worried.

"Josh will go, and so will Naomi's *mamm*," Isaac replied, "so please don't worry."

"Where is Naomi?" Becca asked.

"She's just packing a bag," Isaac answered.

"A bag? Will she be away for a while?"

"We're not sure," Isaac said. "But she just wants to be prepared in case she has to stay over at the hospital."

"I certainly hope it's not that serious," Becca remarked with a slight shiver.

"I'll walk you home," Isaac said, after Becca had seen Naomi off.

"We're just next door," Becca replied, "I'll be alright."

"I insist," Isaac said.

"You know, there are times when I wish we had telephones. Like now, when we need to know what's going on with Naomi," Becca declared.

"Actually, I asked Josh to call the phone booth, and I am going over to wait there with my sisters, Maria and Anna," Isaac replied, "so I can tell you when we hear something."

"Won't it be freezing cold at the phone booth?" Becca asked.

"Have you been there lately?" Isaac laughed. "It's now housed in a café that stays open all night, especially so that we can use the phone and receive calls during emergencies."

"What is the café called?" Becca queried. "And no, I haven't heard of this new development."

"The Maple Tree," Isaac answered.

"I know The Maple Tree," Becca remarked, "and I've even eaten there. But it never had a phone booth."

"That's obviously a recent development," Isaac replied.

"Well then, if you would give me a few minutes to get ready and to request my *mamm* to watch our boys, may I come with you? Naomi is my best friend, you see, and I would like to know what's happening with her," Becca said. "That's why I was hoping to go to the hospital with her."

"It's better that you stayed here to take care of things, Becca," Isaac said gently. "And of course, you may come with us."

Becca looked at Isaac in surprise, realizing that that was probably the first time she had noticed the way he said her name.

"How are we going?" Becca asked.

"I think we can all fit into one buggy," Isaac replied.

Later Becca would remember that night as being strangely confusing, but pleasantly so, as she got to know Anna and Maria Ropp. They sat on either side of her at the café and asked her questions about her life and her family.

"How strange that we never actually talked until this evening," Anna remarked, as a waiter set mugs of hot chocolate before them.

"But that's because you have been so occupied with the children all these past days," Maria observed.

Becca couldn't reveal to Anna and Maria that she always preferred being with the children. When she was with the adults, she felt out of place being a widow at such a young age.

Every so often, during the conversation, Becca would feel Isaac's eyes on her and would turn to look at him, but he would turn away quickly. It seemed like he was trying to figure something out, and she couldn't quite understand what it was.

"Isaac doesn't like gatherings, generally," Maria remarked, seeing Becca glance his way. "Ever since Eva passed, he finds it difficult answering questions about how he manages as a single parent."

"What's to manage?" Isaac countered. "We are Amish. I am fortunate to live right next door to my family, whose help has been invaluable since Simon lost his mother."

"I know what you mean," Becca said. "I didn't want to say so, but gatherings have been hard for me too. But this holiday, with Naomi's family and ours all together, it was far easier than I imagined it would be. And of course, I am so grateful to my family for helping me care for Mark. I don't think I could have done it on my own, being as distraught as I was after losing David."

She bit her lip. "Oh dear," she murmured, "I just realized I have never actually talked about this to anyone but Naomi. Which reminds me, does she have the number of the payphone here?"

"She does, and so does Josh," Isaac answered. "And please, do continue to tell us about yourself and how it has been taking care of Mark on your own."

Becca looked uncertainly at Anna and Maria, and then at Isaac, as all three of them stared back at her enquiringly.

"I have to admit," Becca said, looking down at her cup of hot chocolate, "that every day since David passed has been a challenge that I wouldn't have been able to handle had it not been for Mark. Every day I realize that I derive the strength to go on from him. When he looks at me, I see the reason why I can't give in to my abiding grief."

"I echo the sentiments that you have expressed so beautifully," Isaac declared.

"Mark and Simon have become good friends," Maria remarked. "I am concerned how they will take it when the time comes to say goodbye to each other."

"I try not to think about it," Becca replied. "It's perhaps best to live in the moment."

"The phone's ringing!" Isaac exclaimed, jumping to his feet. "It sure is loud!"

"Wait, Isaac," Anna said, "one of the café staff is going to answer it."

"I want to answer myself. I'm going to see if it's Josh calling from the hospital," Isaac said, hurrying over to the telephone booth. When he stepped into the booth and they could see him with the receiver to his ear, Becca jumped up.

"I need to know what's going on," she said.

"We'll come too," Anna and Maria said, following her as she hurried towards the phone booth in a corner of the café, just as Isaac stepped out, looking puzzled.

"What's wrong?" Becca, Anna and Maria chorused.

"The good news is that Naomi is fine," Isaac answered. "Josh couldn't tell me what was wrong, but just said she was fine, and would be back home tonight."

"That's good news indeed," Becca declared, heaving a sigh of relief.

"But there's a message that Josh said I was to give you, Becca," Isaac continued.

"What is it?" Becca asked, looking troubled again.

"Josh said that Naomi had asked him to tell you that what Mercy Troyer said was true," Isaac answered.

"It is?" Becca whispered. "Well, now, that's the best news ever!"

"What does it mean?" Anna queried.

"Naomi will have to tell you herself," Becca answered, her face breaking into a smile.

CHAPTER FIVE

When Naomi returned from the hospital in the middle of the night, Becca jumped up from her bed and went to the window. She smiled to herself, seeing members of the Ropp family come out to greet her and hearing squeals of excitement as Naomi and Josh could hold their joyful news in no longer.

"You got your wish for the New Year," Becca said excitedly to Naomi when she went over to meet her the next day.

"To think that I had to meet a lady called Mercy Troyer before I went to get myself checked," Naomi remarked. "To be honest, I have felt nauseous quite often in the past weeks, and put it all down to eating too much during the holidays!" She sat down on the chair opposite her friend. "Becca," she said, "I am overjoyed. And I want you to be overjoyed too."

"Naomi, my dear, I am ever so happy for you and Joshua," Becca replied emphatically.

"No, no, Becca, I know you're happy for us. But it's you that I'm talking about. I want you to be overjoyed this New Year too."

"I will be, if we serve the best New Year's Eve supper that we've ever cooked," Becca laughed.

"Supper on New Year's Eve will be wonderful," Naomi declared. "I just know it will." She gave Becca a curious look. "I heard that you were with Isaac, Maria and Anna when Josh called from the hospital," she said. "How was it?"

"How was what?" Becca queried. "We were all anxious about you, and I was grateful to them for so kindly agreeing to take me along with them."

"Oh," Becca murmured, looking disappointed. "You mean you asked if you could go? Didn't Isaac… perhaps… suggest that you do?"

"No," Becca replied. "He just told me that they were going, and I asked if I could join them. I was so worried about you, Naomi."

"Becca," Naomi said, "tell me more about that night at the café."

"We drank hot chocolate, and Anna and Maria wanted to know all about me," Becca answered.

"And Isaac? What did he do while you were talking to his sisters?" Naomi asked.

"Isaac joined in the conversation. He asked questions too. Like how I coped as a single parent. He obviously understood how it felt, because of his own experience," Becca answered. "But why do you ask? Are you concerned about Isaac? Is there something wrong?"

"Becca, have you ever looked at Isaac and thought…" Naomi began, but Isaac walked in just then.

"Did I hear my name being mentioned?" Isaac asked. "*Gute mariye*, Becca," he added.

"*Gute mariye*, Isaac," Becca replied. "I don't suppose you could have got much sleep last night. Or did you manage to?"

"I was going to ask you the same thing," Isaac laughed. "Because Simon and Mark would have woken you up and kept you from getting a few extra hours of sleep."

"No matter what time I sleep, I'm up for my chores," Becca said, "so I might be just a bit drowsy today."

"Well, I hope you're going to join us for the indoor games we have planned," Naomi said anxiously. "For the adults," she added.

"Do I have a choice?" Becca asked, chuckling. "*Gute mariye*, Anna," she said, as Isaac's sister entered the room.

"Hello, Becca," Anna smiled. *"Wie bisht du?"*

"I am well, thank you, and overjoyed for Naomi and Joshua," Becca replied.

"It's wonderful news, to be sure," Anna replied. "Another Ropp will be arriving soon." She turned to Isaac. "Speaking of Ropps," she said, "I hear that Becca has been asked to make pork and sauerkraut for our New Year's Eve supper."

"Why are you looking at me?" Isaac asked with a shrug.

"Because I was told that Becca makes the finest pork and sauerkraut. But I wondered how that could be true, because I know that you, Isaac, make the best pork and sauerkraut I have ever eaten."

"He does?" Naomi queried, leaning forward eagerly.

"I have an idea," Anna said. "Let's have a pork and sauerkraut competition between the Ropps and Weavers—well, between Isaac and Becca, actually."

"That's a splendid idea," Naomi remarked enthusiastically. "It will definitely add some excitement to the night we have planned."

"I don't mind a friendly competition," Becca smiled. "But when are we going to have it? Don't forget we will also be singing hymns and praying together before we count down to the New Year."

"You can each prepare your pork and sauerkraut and bring it in to supper, and then we will ask various family members to judge. Perhaps one from each age group," Naomi suggested.

"I'm not so sure I want to be beaten in a competition," Isaac declared with a laugh. "I'm sure Becca is a far better cook than I could ever hope to be."

"I am impressed that you cook, Isaac," Becca said. "And it would be a lot of fun, I am sure, to have a competition."

"Simon and Mark would love it," Naomi declared.

But, as it happened, Simon and Mark wanted nothing to keep them apart, especially not a competition that would challenge their loyalties. The boys protested, and eventually, Maria had a suggestion.

"I know," she said, when she heard that Simon and Mark were not in favor of any kind of battle between the Ropps and the Weavers, however friendly the battle was to be, "since both Becca and Isaac are so good at preparing the most important dish that is traditionally served at our

New Year's celebration, let there be a collaboration."

"You mean that Becca and Isaac prepare the pork and sauerkraut together?" Naomi asked, her face breaking into a happy smile.

"Yes," Maria answered.

Isaac glanced uncertainly at Becca. "But would that be alright with you, Becca?" he asked. "I'm sure you have your own recipe and I have mine, and I wouldn't want there to be any conflict over ingredients."

"It's a collaboration," Naomi declared. "So place your recipes side by side, and see if you can prepare the dish using the best of both the recipes. How does that sound?"

"It would mean that we won't be sure how it will turn out, and that could be risky," Becca said.

"I think it would work," Isaac declared.

"Alright then," Naomi said. "That's settled." She chuckled. "A Ropp-Weaver collaboration. What could be better?"

"We want to help too," Simon declared firmly. "I want to cook."

"I want to cook too," Mark said.

Becca and Isaac looked helplessly at their families standing around them.

"Of course you can help," Becca said, getting down on her knees to hug both Mark and Simon together. "We'll be a team."

***

Isaac picked up a pail of water and walked into the stables, where Joshua had already begun grooming the buggy horses.

"Here I am," Isaac announced.

"Aren't you supposed to be cooking?" Joshua enquired amusedly.

"That's not till tomorrow when we need to get the pork prepared for the day after," Isaac replied. He gave Joshua a searching look.

"Josh, did you all plan this, by any chance?" he asked.

"Plan what?" Joshua asked.

"The Ropp-Weaver cooking collaboration," Isaac replied, beginning to groom one of the horses.

"No, we didn't plan it, Isaac," Joshua said. "But maybe The Lord did."

"You really think so?" Isaac asked uncertainly. "Because I have tried to gauge Becca's feelings, and I don't think she even truly looks at me. I am just Naomi's cousin to her, and she can never think of me as anything more than that."

"What makes you so sure?" Joshua asked.

"I would know, wouldn't I?" Isaac replied. "I do believe that it's just too soon to expect Becca to forget the husband that she so obviously misses even now, just as I miss my dear Eva. It's hard to think of having anyone else in our lives."

"But you have thought about having Becca in your life, haven't you, Isaac?" Joshua asked.

"I have," Isaac admitted. "I have done nothing but think of how it would be, ever since that day when I watched her in the snow with the children. She is so good with Simon too, and he needs a *mamm*."

"I am sure that Becca would have also thought about Mark having a *daed* again," Joshua remarked.

"Has she said anything to Naomi?" Isaac asked eagerly.

"No, she hasn't… yet," Joshua answered. "But it's only a matter of time."

"Time is something we don't have a lot of, Josh," Isaac murmured. "I leave three days after New Year's Day."

"Then you must talk to Becca, Isaac," Joshua urged.

"I would have done so already if I had any indication that she had some interest in a collaboration other than the pork and sauerkraut one," Isaac laughed despite himself. Then he sighed. "And now I have to think of how Simon will react when it's time to leave Cloverfield Village, where we have all had such a wonderful time."

"Stay on for a while longer, then," Joshua suggested. "You know you are always welcome to do that."

"I might," Isaac said, "if I get some indication that there's any hope of Becca thinking of me as a prospective…"

"Husband?" Joshua completed his sentence. "You can say it, Isaac. I am certain that Eva and David would want you both to be happy, and Simon and Mark to have a complete family."

Isaac shrugged. "Only The Lord knows," he murmured.

"Then we shall pray over this," Joshua said. "That The Lord may speak to Becca and give her a revelation."

"If indeed it is His will that we should change our single parent status," Isaac replied.

"Isaac," Joshua said, setting his grooming brush aside and leaning against the horse's stall.

"Naomi and I had all but given up hope of ever being parents, and yet now, all of a sudden when we least expected it, we have a baby on the way. I can scarce believe it. But it's true. So have faith, Isaac. There's always a divine plan about to unfold."

"I have prayed so much these past days, Josh," Isaac said. "Because loneliness is a very hard thing to bear, and even harder is to watch my son growing up without a mother's arms to hold him." He smiled. "You know, Becca is a wonderful woman. I could see her as Simon's *mamm*. But what frightens me so much is that if I were to ask her and she refused my offer of courtship or marriage, I would be devastated on Simon's account as well as mine."

In the milking shed, Becca huddled by a full pail of milk and stared at it unseeingly. She was thinking of David and the way they had met and married, and the day he had exited her life, so harshly torn from her side by a cruel twist of tragic fate. His passing had left a void too large to bear, and it was only when her days were full, the way that they had been these past weeks, that she could actually enjoy life. Once New Year's Day came and went, when the holidays were behind her and the days just resumed their ordinary pace, then it would again be a time of tossing in her sleep, her face wet with tears, her arms around Mark as he clung to her and asked why every other boy had a *daed* and he didn't. She dropped her head into her arms and began to weep.

"Becca?" a voice called out and she froze.

"Isaac?" she queried, facing away from him. "What brings you here so early in the day?"

"Naomi sent me over with the pork, and your *mamm* said that I would find you here. She asked me to come and fetch you, so that we could begin preparing the meat for the oven."

"Oh," Becca said flatly. "Of course."

"Is there something I can do to help?" Isaac asked gently. "You don't seem to be yourself."

"Actually," Becca said, still facing away from him, "I am myself. This is who I am. Sometimes I cry and sometimes I laugh. I cry when I miss David and wonder how Mark will manage without a *daed* for the rest of his life, and I laugh when I see him happy and when there are things happening around me that make me smile." She dried her eyes on her apron and stood up. "I'm sorry. I don't mean to be dramatic. But honestly, I have to admit—life is hard."

"I know," Isaac replied. "I understand better than you think I do."

"You're in the same position, I know," Becca said, turning to him and beginning to cry again. "Do you have any advice for me?"

"I do, actually," Isaac ventured hesitantly.

"Please tell me," Becca said, dragging the back of her hand across her eyes. "Because soon New Year's Day will be past us and the normal pace of life will be upon us, and I just cannot bear the emptiness of it." She bit her lip so hard it turned red. "I'm sorry. I don't mean to sound ungrateful. I am fortunate to have my family who loves me and dotes on Mark…"

"Becca," Isaac said. "You don't have to apologize for feeling the way you do and for voicing your pain. In fact, I'm glad you are talking about it. It makes me feel less alone to know that you're going through what I am going through. It's no different for a man than it is for a woman, you know. The problems are the same. The loneliness is the same. And the concern for one's child is the same. I worry about Simon too. What will his state of mind be when we have to leave Cloverfield in a few days, and how will he go through all the rest of his life without a *mamm*?"

"I'm sorry if I raked up sad memories," Becca said. "This is a happy time, and we have so much to be grateful for. Naomi's news, for instance."

"Becca," Isaac said, "you don't have to apologize for feeling sorrow. You are justified, you know, and it's alright."

Becca stifled a sob, and forced a weak smile onto her face.

"We have pork to prepare for the oven," she said shakily. "Let's go and get started."

CHAPTER SIX

"Mark, Simon," Isaac instructed the two boys, "your job is to rub the salt well into the pork."

"And then sprinkle the herbs over the meat," Becca said.

"But I never use herbs when I cook pork," Isaac remarked.

"Well, in this collaboration, we have to use ingredients from both recipes, hence the herbs," Becca declared, flashing Isaac a smile.

She gave him a covert look as he worked on the pork, flanked by Mark and Simon. He was fully dressed in his traditional Amish clothes, down to the hat on his head, yet completely at home in the kitchen.

"When did you learn how to cook?" Becca asked.

"When I became a single parent. I decided I would cook for Simon, rather than have my *mamm* send food over," Isaac replied.

"I'm cooking!" Mark squealed joyfully.

"I'm cooking too!" Simon announced, as both the boys vigorously rubbed salt into the pork and sprinkled the herbs over the meat. As more salt and herbs flew over the kitchen floor than onto the meat, causing much mirth, Isaac and Becca's eyes met as they shared a moment of silent understanding.

Soon the pork was placed in the oven, and they stood back, all four of them talking and laughing companionably. And when members of their families took furtive peeks into the kitchen, they nodded knowingly at each other and exchanged secretive smiles as they discussed the Ropp-Weaver collaboration.

The next day, on New Year's Eve, the pork and sauerkraut were laid out on a large platter at the very center of the table along with an assortment of pies that Becca and Isaac had baked together with their sons. After the feast, as hymns were sung and prayers for the New Year were prayed, Becca felt an unfamiliar yet pleasant stirring in her heart. She looked up, and her eyes met Isaac's across the room as her pulse quickened. A stab of guilt momentarily overwhelmed her, but then she felt her mother's arm around her shoulders as she whispered to her that it was time she let go of her pain. She could never forget David and would never get over him, but The Lord had presented a way. There was no guilt in opening her heart again to welcome a love that could give Mark a *daed* and Simon a *mamm*.

And then Naomi came over to her and echoed her mother's words.

"But Isaac hasn't said anything or indicated that he feels the way you say he does," Becca whispered to Naomi.

"If he does," Naomi said, "promise me that you will consider what he has to say."

There was still a while to go till midnight, and more games were laid out. Becca once again found herself immersed in taking care of the children and, for a while, forgot what her mother and Naomi had said. Isaac was with the menfolk in another room, when suddenly Becca realized that she found herself missing his presence. It was a strange feeling. She had spent so much time in his company in the past few days, and suddenly he wasn't there. And then, even as she found herself missing him, he appeared in the room with Joshua. Naomi ran to Joshua's side and took his hand.

The countdown was only minutes away. Husbands sought their wives while children clustered around their parents, and Becca looked for her family and found them all in pairs. She took Mark's hand in hers and held it tight, when she suddenly felt someone tugging at her other hand. It was Simon.

"Oh, Simon, my little one," Becca whispered, taking his hand in hers. And then, from across the room, Isaac approached, hesitantly at first and then more purposefully.

"Becca," Isaac said, "I guess we are the odd ones out, so may I join you?"

"Of course," Becca replied, feeling a sense of relief wash over her.

"Actually, there's something I need to say," Isaac said, leaning closer and raising his voice slightly above the buzz of conversation in the lamplit room.

"What is it?" Becca asked.

"The Ropp-Weaver collaboration," Isaac said, "would you consider taking it further?"

As Becca turned to him in surprise, Isaac continued, "For our sons? And for us too? Please?"

For the first time, Becca noticed that Isaac had the most expressive eyes, and they were speaking to her with an eloquence that required no words. She also realized something else. She was feeling a sense of joyful anticipation even as the assembled company of Ropps and Weavers counted down to the New Year.

"I do like the idea of a collaboration," Becca said, above the sound of people wishing each other a Happy New Year.

Isaac found her hand and held it to his lips. She saw Mark and Simon smiling at each other. Now there would be no goodbyes.

"I asked the Lord for a brother for Christmas," Simon shouted, "and He gave me one!"

"And He is also giving you a *mamm*," Isaac said.

"And a *daed* for you, Mark," Becca whispered into her son's ear.

And then the greetings for the New Year turned into congratulations and wishes for their happiness, and Naomi began to suggest wedding dates which would ensure that her baby would be there for the occasion. As more plans were made and thus, as the holidays came to an end, Becca realized that she was left with a feeling of quiet contentment and that the void was filled. Stranger still was that she looked at Isaac now and felt a warmth she hadn't thought she would ever feel for another man. And in his eyes, she saw unquestionable love.

"I never thought it would be possible to love again," Becca whispered to him. "But I need to tell you, so that you know that I am not only marrying you to give Mark a *daed*. The fact is, I love you, Isaac Ropp."

"And I you, Becca, from the first day to the last."

The End

Please Check out My Other Works

By checking out the link below

http://cleanromancepublishing.com/rbauth

Thank You

Many thanks for taking the time to buy and read through this book.

It means lots to be supported by SPECIAL readers like YOU.

Hope you enjoyed the book; please support my writing by leaving an honest review to assist other readers.

.

With Regards,

Ruth Bawell